This book is dedicated to
Caitlin, Annalise, Christopher, James,
William, Abigail, Avery and Sienna.

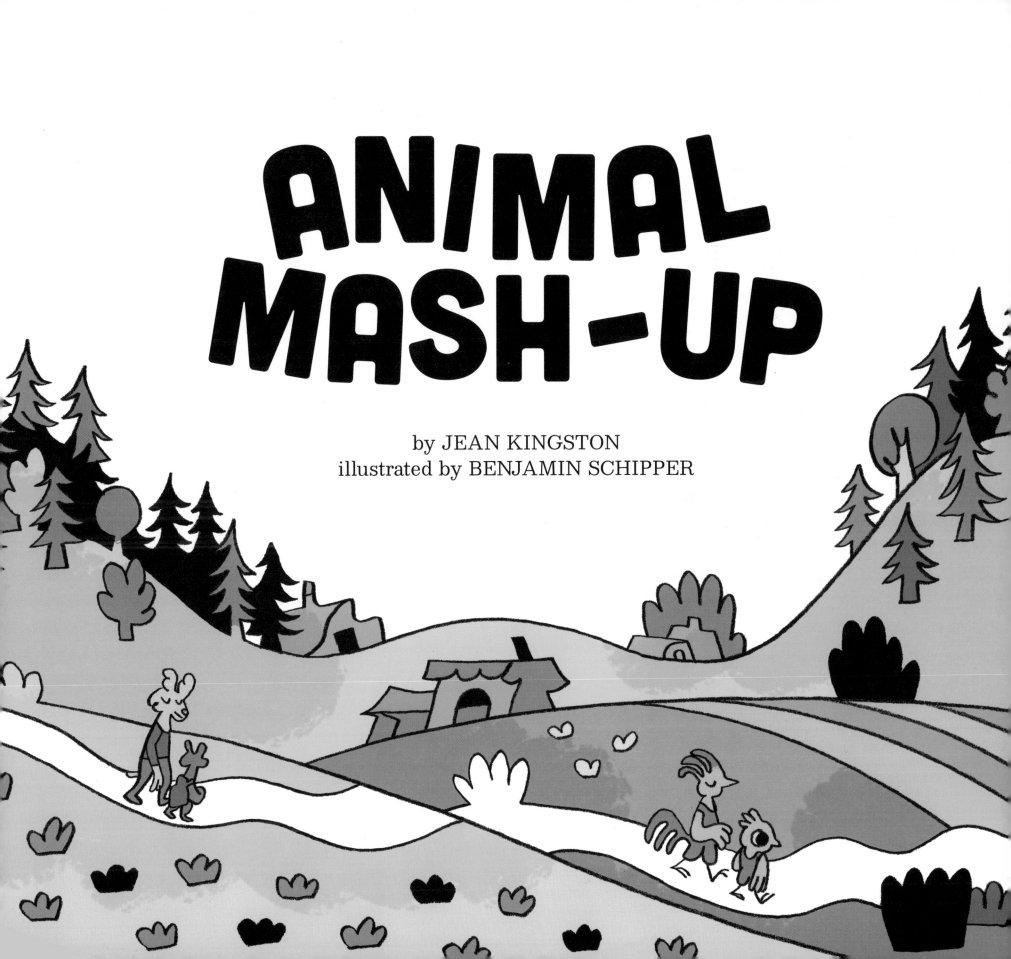

ANIMAL MASH-UP

by JEAN KINGSTON

illustrated by BENJAMIN SCHIPPER

In Farmville, dogs went to Dog School.
Alpacas went to Alpaca School.
Goats went to Goat School.

Some schools were too crowded.

The slide had a traffic jam. Lunch lines were so long, students had to eat cold, rubbery pizza. They always ran out of crayons.

Other schools were too empty.

One goat had seven parts in the play. Two alpacas made up the jazz quartet. Three frustrated cows tried to play four square.

Town leaders had an idea.

"Let's put the animals together. Class sizes will be perfect!"

They cheered.

However, the students whined, complained, and grumbled.

Baxter Beagle howled, "Goats are messy! Alpacas are odd!"

Chelsey Chicken clucked, "I'll miss my best friends."

Shelly Sheep bleated, "Only sheep know how to play Wool Ball."

Teacher Henry Hoof worried Animal Mash-Up School would flop. All summer, he noodled over the problem.

Baxter and his best friend, Penny Poodle, walked together on the first day of school.

From across the street, Gordy Goat taunted, "Sit, Baxter! Sit, Penny!! Good dogs!" His friends snickered. "Rollover! Fetch!"

"Goats!" Baxter mumbled. "Never liked them, never will."

In class, Baxter and Penny
sat together.

The goats chanted, "Goats go
with goats! Goats go with goats!"

The cows joined, "Cows go with cows!
Cows go with cows!"

Sam Sloth, who had just moved to Farmville,
quietly sat alone.

"BOOM, BOOM, WHOMP-A-WHOMP!" Mr. Hoof hushed the class with his drums. "Our school's success depends on cooperation and kindness."

"Dream on," Gordy muttered.

"Excuse me?" asked Mr. Hoof.

"I'm all about kindness," said Gordy with pretend sweetness.

"That's the spirit, Gordy!"

Baxter rolled his eyes, while Penny frowned.

Mr. Hoof said, "Let's start with the
Opinion Game. Grab a button!"

"Chocolate or vanilla cupcakes?"

They placed their button under their favorite flavor.

Everyone liked cupcakes, except Abby, Annie and Alden, the alpaca triplets.

"We prefer blueberry pie à la mode!"

Baxter, Penny, and Gordy liked vanilla cupcakes, along with Mr. Hoof, Sam, and Chelsey.

"Surprise!" exclaimed Mr. Hoof.

He presented them with a big platter of cupcakes.

Gordy popped one into his mouth.
"That's a one-biter! May I have another?"

"Sure can, but don't get used to this," Mr. Hoof said
with a toothy grin.

When the triplets joined the cupcake party,
the class cheered.

Mr. Hoof began the next day with
the Opinion Game.

"Pop music or country music?"

"Country music!" said Baxter, Penny,
and Gordy in unison.

They laughed. Their opinions
matched again.

Before sitting back down, Shelly and Baxter
grabbed guitars. The alpacas danced.
Penny sang. Mr. Hoof blew on his saxophone,
while Sam played the piano.

Gordy watched, tapping his hooves.

Who knew sheep strummed, alpacas had fancy
feet and dogs belted out songs? Who knew horses
played jazz and sloths had fast fingers?
Together, they had created their own musical
mash-up!

However, something was missing.

"Join us, Gordy!" said Penny.

Instead, he ran away.

They followed and found Gordy wiping away tears. Penny hugged him.

"Mom just had babies," sniffled Gordy. "Everything is about bottles and diapers. The fridge is empty. My brothers broke my drums. Nobody cares."

"We can help," said Penny.

"We'll sell our wool and get your drum fixed!" said the sheep.
"I can play catch with your brothers," said Baxter.
"I'm an expert at egg casseroles," said Chelsey.
"I can hang with you," said Sam.
"And we can...knit you warm sweaters!" added the alpacas.

Gordy smiled. "I'm sorry I've been a grumpy goat."

"We're stronger together,"
said Mr. Hoof.

"Friends go with friends!
Friends go with friends!"
they chanted all the way back
to Mr. Hoof's room.

"Take these drumsticks!" Baxter said.

Gordy's face beamed. They continued their
Animal Mash-Up song.

This time, it was perfect.

When the last note ended, the class played the Opinion Game.

Animal Mash-Up School or Same Animal School?"

The pile of buttons under "Animal Mash-Up School" overflowed.

The class cheered.

AME ANIMAL SCHOOL
ANIMAL MASH-UP SCHOOL
BAXTER
PENNY
DOUG
GORDY
ABBY
MR HOOF
LOU
CHELSEY
SAM
ALDEN

"Don't get used to this!" said Mr. Hoof with a toothy grin.

Out came cupcakes AND blueberry pie ā la mode.

"One-biters and pie for everyone!" shouted Gordy, before stuffing his mouth...again.

No one can whistle a symphony. It takes a whole orchestra to play it.
- H. E. Luccock

Alone we can do so little; together we can do so much.
- Helen Keller